MARC BROWN

ARTHUR'S
PET BUSINESS

1837

Little, Brown and Company
Boston   New York   Toronto   London

For Stan and Bill Eloranta,
who helped make my new treehouse studio happen.
M.B.

First Paperback Edition

Library of Congress Cataloging-in-Publication Data

Brown, Marc Tolon.
  Arthur's pet business/Marc Brown. — 1st ed.
    p.   cm.
  Summary: Arthur's determination to prove he is responsible enough
to have a puppy brings him a menagerie of animals to care for.
  ISBN 0-316-11262-3 (hc)
  ISBN 0-316-11316-6 (pb)
  [1. Dogs. — Fiction. 2. Pets — Fiction. 3. Anteaters — Fiction.]
I. Title.
PZ7.B81618Arm   1990
[E] — dc20   89-26991
                                                              CIP
                                                               AC

10 9 8 7

WOR

Published simultaneously in Canada
by Little, Brown & Company (Canada) Limited

Printed in the United States of America

"You've been looking at puppies for months,"
said D.W.
"When are you going to ask Mom and Dad
if you can have one?"
"I'm waiting for just the right moment,"
said Arthur, "so promise not to say anything!"

That night at dinner, Father asked,
"What's new?"
"Arthur wants a puppy," said D.W.
"Blabbermouth!" said Arthur.

"A puppy is a big responsibility," said Father.
"I can take care of it," said Arthur.
"We'll think about it," Mother said.
"That means no," explained D.W.

After dinner Mother and Father did the dishes.
"Can you hear what they're saying?" asked Arthur.
"They're worried about the new carpet," whispered D.W.
Suddenly the door opened.

"We've decided you may have a puppy if you can take care of it," said Father.

"Wow!" said Arthur.

"*But,*" said Mother, "first you need to show us you're responsible."

"How will I ever prove I'm responsible?" asked Arthur.
"The best way I know is to get a job," said D.W.
"Then you can pay back the seven dollars you owe me!"
"Ka-chingg!" went her cash register.

Arthur wondered what kind of
job he could do.
"You could work for my dad
at the bank," said Muffy.
"He needs some new tellers."

"If I were you, I'd get a job
at Joe's Junk Yard crushing
old cars," offered Binky Barnes.

"Do something that *you* like,"
said Francine.
That gave Arthur an idea.

"I'll take care of other people's pets," said Arthur,
"then Mom and Dad will know I can take care
of my own."

Arthur and Francine put up signs to advertise
his new business.

His family helped, too.

Arthur waited and waited. Then, just before bedtime, the phone rang.

"Hello," he said. "Arthur's Pet Business. How may I help you?

"Yes. No. When? Where? Great!" said Arthur.

"Hooray! I'm going to watch Mrs. Wood's dog while she's on vacation, and I'll earn ten dollars!"
"Oh, no!" said D.W. "Not nasty little Perky?"
"Isn't that the dog the mailman calls 'JAWS'?" asked Father.
"That's Perky!" said D.W.

The next morning, Arthur ran all the way to
Mrs. Wood's house.
"Right on time!" said Mrs. Wood.
"*Grrrrr,*" growled Perky.

"She hasn't been herself lately," said Mrs. Wood.
"I'm worried."
"I'll take good care of her," said Arthur.
"We'll be best friends."
"*Grrrrr,*" growled Perky.
"Here's her schedule and a list of things
she doesn't like," said Mrs. Wood.
"I'll see you next Sunday."

Arthur did his best to make
Perky feel at home.
Every day he brushed her.
He tried to fix her
favorite foods.
They took lots of long walks —
day and night.
Perky made sure they had the whole
sidewalk to themselves.

"You look exhausted," said Mother. "Maybe taking care of a dog is too much work . . ."
"Any dog I get will be easier than Perky," said Arthur.

Word of Arthur's pet business got around.
On Monday the MacMillans asked Arthur to watch
their canary, Sunny.

On Tuesday Prunella gave Arthur
her ant farm.

On Wednesday the Brain asked
Arthur to take care of his frogs
while he went on vacation.

Best of all, on Thursday The Amazing Larry
asked Arthur to keep Cuddles,
his trained boa constrictor.

Animals were everywhere
— until Mother put her foot down.
"I want all these animals in the basement *now!*"
she ordered.

By bedtime all the pets were downstairs.
All except Perky.
Perky slept in Arthur's room.

On Saturday Buster asked Arthur to go to the movies. "I can't," said Arthur. "When I finish cleaning these cages, it will be feeding time.

"And anyway, it's Perky's last night with me and she seems sick. I don't want to leave her."

"Well, I bet you're happy today," said D.W.
the next morning.
"You get rid of Perky and collect ten dollars!"
"I can't believe it," said Arthur.
"But I'm going to miss Perky."

"Arthur, Mrs. Wood just called to say she's
on her way over," said Mother.
"Now, wait here, Perky," ordered Arthur.
"I'll go and get your leash."

When Arthur went back into the kitchen,
Perky was gone.
"Here Perky! Perky!" called Arthur.
But Perky didn't come.
"She's not in the basement," called Father.
"She's not in the backyard," said D.W.
"She's lost!" said Arthur.
"Oh, oh!" said D.W. "You're in big trouble!"

"Arthur, Mrs. Wood is here!" called Mother.

"Hi, Mrs. Wood," said D.W. "Guess what?
Arthur lost Perky!"

"My poor little darling is lost?" asked Mrs. Wood.

"Don't worry," said Father. "Arthur's looking for
her right now."

Suddenly they heard a bark.

"Everybody come quick!" called Arthur.

"Look," said Arthur. "Perky's had puppies!"
"No wonder she's been acting so strange,"
said Mrs. Wood.
"You've done a wonderful job taking care of Perky,
when she needed a friend the most.
How can I ever thank you?"

"A reward might be nice," suggested D.W.

"Shush!" said Mother.

"Here's the money I owe you," said Mrs. Wood.

"And, how would you like to keep one of Perky's puppies as a special thank you?"

"I'd love to," said Arthur. "If I'm allowed."

"Of course," said Mother. "You've earned it."

"Wow!" said Arthur.
"Ten dollars *and* my very own puppy!
I can't believe it!"
"Neither can I," said D.W. "Now you can finally pay
back my seven dollars."
"Ka-chingg!" went her cash register.